JONNY BRIGGS
AND THE GALLOPING WEDDING

JONNY BRIGGS
and the
GALLOPING WEDDING

Joan Eadington

Illustrated by William Marshall

as told in Jackanory by
Bernard Holley

BBC/KNIGHT

Copyright © Joan Eadington 1983
Illustrations © British Broadcasting Corporation 1983
First published 1983 by British Broadcasting
Corporation/Knight Books
Third impression 1983

British Library C.I.P.

Eadington, Joan
    Jonny Briggs and the galloping wedding.–
    (Knight books)
I. Title   II. Marshall, William
    823′.914[J] P27

ISBN 0 340 33022 8
        (0 563 20139 8 BBC)

*The characters and situations in this book are entirely imaginary and bear
no relation to any real person or actual happening*

This book is sold subject to the condition that it shall not, by
way of trade or otherwise, be lent, re-sold, hired out or otherwise
circulated without the publisher's prior consent in any form of
binding or cover other than that in which it is published and
without a similar condition including this condition being
imposed on the subsequent purchaser.

Printed and bound in Great Britain for the British Broadcasting
Corporation, 35 Marylebone High Street, London W1M 4AA
and Hodder and Stoughton Paperbacks, a division of Hodder
and Stoughton Ltd., Mill Road, Dunton Green, Sevenoaks,
Kent (Editorial Office: 47 Bedford Square, London, WC1 3DP)
by Richard Clay (The Chaucer Press) Ltd, Bungay, Suffolk

Typeset by Phoenix Photosetting, Chatham

Contents

1
The Unlucky Horseshoe

Jonny Briggs's eyelids were drooping lower and lower. But there was a bit of a smile on his face. He was having a beautiful dream.

He was riding the Horse of the Year. It was brown and white. And Pam was walking along next to him holding a gold plate for the horse's favourite carrot-flavoured sugar lumps.

Dreams are funny things, and even though Jonny knew he was fast asleep he also knew it was better than just sitting in Miss Broom's class listening to her go on and on about weddings. "And now I want you all to draw *your* idea of a wedding!" said Miss Broom in a sharp, clear voice. It woke him up like the pop of a balloon . . .

His idea of a wedding? He looked round the class; everyone was wide awake and talking.

"My aunty had one with twenty-two brides-maids," said Josie, one of the twins. Then catching Jonny's look of disbelief she added: "And there was this horrible page there with short bristly hair dressed in yellow velvet. And he'd got chocolate spilt all down his front and he stood on my aunty's train and ripped it to shreds. It looked like a torn old curtain."

The whole class seemed to hiccup. Nobody believed a word.

Then Jinny, the other twin, said: "Please miss – can we have an extra big piece of paper to draw all the bridesmaids on?"

Greedy swanks . . . trust them to boast the most

and get the most.

"Can I have an extra big piece of paper, too, miss?" said Jonny suddenly. "I want to draw a wedding with horses." He gave them a bland stare then opened his mouth wide like a gorilla and was *almost* going to scratch under his armpits as well until he caught Miss Broom's eye. So instead he smiled meekly at Miss Broom and said in a low, half-ashamed voice: "My sister's getting married in a horse and carriage."

Immediately the class was in an uproar of excitement. What a lie! The Briggs family with horses and carriages?

"Horse and *cart* with goldfish bowls on it, you mean," babbled the twins, angry at being outdone. "And anyway, you can't even draw. Don't give him extra paper, miss! He'll only use it to make paper darts. He tells whoppers all the time. Take no notice!"

"What sort of a carriage?" shouted the Brown brothers. "A *train* carriage like the one where all those hens live, in that scrappy old field?"

Jonny felt himself going pink and prickly. He should never have told them. He wished he could shrivel up and hide in a desk like an apple core. A carriage . . . yes, it did sound unbelievable. At first he could hardly bring himself to say the word carriage. It sounded so unbelievable and daft. But now he was getting used to the idea.

Taking a deep breath and staring defiantly all

round the class, he said: "It's a proper carriage from olden days with red seats inside and a black hood like a big pram. A man's started hiring it out. My sister's his first customer." Jonny felt a sudden surge of pride, and a sympathetic ripple of respect rustled round the room. Everyone was interested now and even a bit envious. Fancy all that rabble with a horse and carriage. ... Fancy a carriage, down scruffy old Port Street, instead of an ordinary wedding car with white sheets on the seats.

Even Miss Broom seemed impressed. She told Jonny to give her very best wishes for the future to his sister Pat. Then she told them all to stop talking and to get on with their work.

Jonny felt like a star now. Everyone was on his side.

"Please miss, have you got any pictures of horses I could trace? It's very hard to draw horses."

Miss Broom hesitated: "It isn't supposed to be a tracing lesson," she said. "I don't mind you tracing some things ... like maps of the world or Highway Code signs ..." She softened: "Have you *got* to have a horse in the picture?"

"Oh yes, miss. There's got to be a horse. It's all arranged for next Saturday morning at St Anne's Church."

The place began to buzz again. Jonny Briggs's sister Pat – the one that did ice-skating – on a horse, and Jonny Briggs sat at the back of her in a black pram – and their Albert in a big tall hat like a chim-

ney-pot . . . Everyone began to giggle.

"That will *do*," called Miss Broom. "Silence! Peter will hand out the drawing paper." Miss Broom was looking stern, now, the few seconds of fame were over: "And Jonny Briggs will have to make up a wedding without a horse on it if he isn't willing to try and draw one without tracing it. None of us is a horse expert but there is such a thing as *trying* to do things."

She went on: "I'm just going to class five to have a word with Mr Hobbs about the faulty heating system, and by the time I get back I expect to see some really good pictures. People doing the very best ones will be allowed to re-do them on decent paper and we'll put their pictures on the wall next to the blackboard." Then Miss Broom hurried away with her head down – in case any hands started to go up.

Jonny sighed. Fancy having to draw something again just because it was good. And not even being allowed to trace it. Just imagine trying to get something right – twice in a row!

Peter started to hand out sheets of paper. It was so thin that it left holes and smears and rough bits if you tried to rub out on it. And it was lucky no one ever had really sharp pencils because sharp pencils prodded it to bits. Only soft, gentle felt-tipped pens could deal with that thin paper, and Pam's were at home. And the last lot ever seen in the Briggs family were now dried out stumps stuck in the backyard to mark out where dad's cabbage seeds were planted.

Everybody was sitting there looking impatiently at Peter as he slowly handed out the paper. "Give us some to hand out," said both the Brown brothers, pushing forward to get at the paper. Peter handed them some and they started to fling it out so quickly that half of it fell on the floor, and everyone began to complain as cries of "I don't want *that* mucky piece after your big clobbering feet have walked all over it," and "I haven't got any," filled the air.

Reluctantly, Jonny bent down and rescued a thin, slightly crumpled sheet from the floor. He knew where this thin paper came from. There was a never-ending roll of it on top of the cupboards in the corridor near Mr Badger's room, marked GENERAL PURPOSES PAPER.

While he was thinking about it, he suddenly thought of something else, too. Something lying right next to the roll of paper on top of the cupboard in a half-hidden place of honour.

It was an old iron horseshoe from the last

carthorse ever to cross the transporter bridge. It was given to Mr Badger as a Christmas present last year by Martin Canebender in case Mr Badger should accidentally give him the slipper for stealing a crate of school milk which he said he never did – which was true – because Mr Hobbs had got the milk numbers added up wrong on his new calculator.

The only thing the famous horseshoe was used for now was to do "rubbings". And you could do "rubbings" really well with the thin paper. You just put bits of things underneath it like bits of tree bark, or a two-penny piece, or a Sheriff's badge, and rubbed the top with a wax crayon. And the shape underneath would come up through the crayon like magic.

As for the horseshoe . . . well, Jonny had never had a chance to use it, but he'd seen some very good knobbly looking shapes of horseshoe made from it by class three . . . And horseshoes were always at weddings – even if they were tiny silver ones made of cardboard. What he needed then – at this very moment – was that horseshoe to make a wedding picture. Instead of trying to draw a *horse*, he could do a rubbing of a horseshoe, instead.

"As soon as Miss Broom gets back," he whispered to Pam, "I'm going to ask her if I can use that old horseshoe to make a proper wedding picture. I'll do it in red crayon and write 'Good Luck, Pat' on it. Then I'll ask Miss Broom if I can take it home." He felt happy at last.

Pam's eyes sparkled: "What a good idea!" she breathed excitedly. She was drawing a bride with sixty-four buttons all of different colours and patterns on a very, very long bride's dress. "Are you going to put anything else on it?"

Jonny shook his head in peaceful bliss, and sat there watching everybody else absorbed in scribbling and drawing, rubbing out, scratching, smoothing, crayoning and felt-tipping. He would have the shape of a real horseshoe on *his* paper. Nothing more, nothing less. "It would spoil it if I had anything else," he said.

"But suppose Miss Brown comes back and sees you sitting here not doing *anything?* Supposing she finds . . . nothing?" Pam looked grave. She began to twiddle a finger through some strands of her brown shiny hair. "Couldn't you even just do a sort of border all round the paper with little dots or something?" Then her face lit up a bit and she said: "You can even make patterns with finger-marks . . ."

"That horseshoe from the top of the cupboard won't need dots, or finger-marks round it —" his words were suddenly drowned . . .

"THAT HORSESHOE FROM MR BADGER'S CUPBOARD?" In a flash, like a great surging wave, the words were rescued and picked up and flung like huge boulders at the heads of the rest of the class.

And Jinny was one of the first to be struck. She stopped drawing. Her ears flapping, her tongue

wagging like a long piece of floppety seaweed, "Did you hear *that?*" she cried out. "He's going to use that horseshoe from Mr Badger's cupboard! That horseshoe is Martin Canebender's. If Martin Canebender wasn't away with chicken-pox he'd –"

"It is *not* Martin Canebender's, Miss Clever-Clogs-Know-All," yelled Pam. "Martin Cane-bender gave it to Mr Badger, and Mr Badger gave it to the school. It belongs to everyone! Mr Badger was very pleased when class three kept using it. He said he was *glad to see it wasn't there to see*, so there!"

The whole class stopped working and began to talk. "When is a horseshoe not a horseshoe?" and "Should horseshoes be seen and not heard, or heard and not seen?" Ten people hadn't even seen it. Three people didn't even know what horseshoes *were*, and three more said, "They're brass door knockers, stupid." Then Lily Spencer put everyone right. First she said her mother was a nurse, then she said horseshoes were made of rusty iron and covered in mud, and that this one came off a scrap heap and had to be dipped in a bucket of disinfectant before it was put on the cupboard. And while all this pandemonium was going on, Nadine, who was usually as quiet as dandelion fluff, was shouting at the top of her voice that Martin Canebender hadn't got chicken-pox at all, "He's left to go to another school," she shrieked, "at LLANFAIR-PWLLGWYNGYLL in Wales . . ." Then she shouted the long word again because her uncle had just taught it to her and she knew no one else could possibly say it properly, because it took a lot of practice.

And at that moment – in walked Miss Broom with Mr Hobbs . . . The noise suddenly faded like a whisp of mist as people slid deep into their seats, including Nadine who was now scarlet, and started to crayon the whole of her picture blue in nervous panic.

"Why are you wriggling about, boy!" Immediately, Mr Hobbs looked straight at Jonny.

"Please sir, my pencil rolled on the floor, sir."

"There'll be more than a *pencil* rolling on the floor, if you don't watch out!" Jonny felt himself go pale and weak as he stared at Mr Hobbs' grey and black check pullover. Not trouble again! Not with Mr Hobbs! And . . . *please save me from ever having to go in his class. Amen.*

"He's your culprit, Miss Broom," said Mr Hobbs, looking as if he had just discovered Australia. "That's the boy behind all this row . . ."

Why did Mr Hobbs always pick on him? He, Jonny Briggs, was the only one being quiet and doing *nothing*. Just sitting. Not even sniffing or scratching his leg. Just waiting patiently for Miss Broom to come back . . .

Then, to his heartfelt relief, Miss Broom gave a polite little cough, smiled back at Mr Hobbs and asked him to feel the hot water pipes to check whether the heating was working properly. And to his amazement, Mr Hobbs actually smiled back and gave a sort of strange strangulated chuckle because he was an expert on hot water pipes – but only when Mr Box wasn't around.

When Mr Hobbs had gone, Miss Broom said: "Right. I'm coming round now, to see what the wedding pictures are like."

Slowly she began to walk all round the class, looking hard at everyone's work.

"You've worked really hard, in spite of all that noise," she said delightedly: "I'm quite proud –"

Then she stopped dead. "Jonny Briggs. What on

earth is this?"

"What, miss?"

"This blank piece of paper."

"Nothing miss . . ."

"I can see it's *nothing*. Have you been asleep?"

As soon as she said this, two large snores filled the air.

"That is *not* funny," said Miss Broom. Then, turning to Pam, she said: "Pamela Dean — you are the after-dinner window monitor. Open all the small windows and let's have some fresh air immediately. Fresh air cures all snores. We shall then, perhaps, be able to find out why someone in this class still has a blank piece of drawing paper in front of them."

She looked hard at Jonny. There was dead silence. "Where is your wedding picture?"

"It's not ready yet, miss . . . Miss Broom." He felt all comfort drain away as the thunder gathered round the small square of blank, white drawing paper on his desk.

"Do you mean to say you've spent the whole of this lesson just doing *nothing?*"

"No miss — I mean yes miss, but —"

"And you were the boy who was going on about drawing a special wedding with horses . . ."

Miss Broom's eyes were like spiky tin-openers.

"I was waiting for you to come back . . ."

"Waiting for *me?* Everyone in the class has worked well without waiting for me! Except you."

"He's been talking, too, miss," said Josie in a loud triumphant voice. "Talking about getting that horseshoe off Mr Badger's cupboard. We're not supposed to take things off cupboards, are we Miss Broom?"

Jonny looked round desperately. "I wasn't going to *take* it. I was going to *ask*. That was why —" But his explanation was drowned. The bell for play-time was ringing. It was very loud. Everyone relaxed. They began to put away their pens and pencils.

Except for Miss Broom still standing there. She didn't relax. "I shall expect to see your wedding picture by first thing tomorrow morning," she said grimly. Then she walked to the door and told them all to get into a straight line.

Jonny knew she meant what she said. "Can I take the paper home with me and do it there, miss?"

As all the rest scuffled out of the classroom, Miss Broom nodded silently. Then she said in her sternest, strictest voice: "And no forgetting," as she marched out of the classroom to do play-ground duty.

"Cheer up Jonny," said Pam when they were in the yard. "You're lucky in a way. You'll be able to do a really good one at home. You'll have as long as you like, and lots of space. And the twins won't be there – an' –"

"You don't know our house," said Jonny dolefully. Then, brightening up, he said: "Humph might show me how to draw a horse though . . .!"

"And I'll get you my felt-tipped pens at dinner time, but see you don't leave the tops off them." They smiled at each other.

That afternoon as he hurried back home after school with Pam's pens grasped firmly in an old paper bag along with the drawing paper, he began to feel quite excited.

Perhaps in the end, his would be the best wedding picture ever! A real Briggs wedding picture about a real Briggs wedding. He might even draw himself in the picture, with his gold belt on.

He began to race to the top of Port Street. Then he stopped in complete and sudden amazement. For outside his own front door, standing there peacefully in the late summer air, was a large brown and white pony. And everyone was standing round staring at it and smiling and talking.

He began to run quickly again, towards home.

2
Disappearing Acts

"Fancy calling a horse like that 'Hurricane'," sniffed Rita jealously as they all drifted into the house with sounds of horse's hooves clopping away in the distance. "If *I* get married . . . if there is someone good enough with a proper sense of humour instead of some of these people like the ones round here whose faces nearly crack with the effort of pretending to be nice to me and Mavis . . . *I* shall have a proper grey Rolls Royce. And none of those old coke tins clanging on the back either. If I ever –"

"Your turn will come, lass," said dad dryly. "But meanwhile it's our Pat's turn."

"Yes," said Pat, who looked a bit pale and peaky, "and if you don't mind it's a *pony*."

"So that's what it was!" said Albert cheerfully, guzzling the last tea-cake out of a crumpled paper bag. "Fancy being dragged to a wedding by a rocking-horse with a name like Snooker."

Pat's eyes began to flash: "Ponies may be small but they aren't rocking-horses. And its name's Hurricane not Snooker. And I don't care if *none* of you come to our wedding. You're an ignorant, hateful, horrible lot and the sooner I change my name the better!"

And she dashed upstairs to have a cry with such a strange sort of agonised howl that Jonny thought it sounded like a ship's hooter on a foggy night.

"I've never known our Pat cry so much," said mam sighing. "Our Pat was the happiest girl alive when she and Dale were doing ice-skating and not getting married."

"Because she was never in to be got at," said Humph calmly. "The more you stay surrounded by people like our Albert and Rita, the more chance there is of tears coming to the eyes."

Jonny agreed with him. He agreed with them all, really. He'd never thought weddings would make people *cry* all the time. They certainly made some people, like dad, yawn . . . Dad was always yawning and scratching his nose and looking for a can of ale when they went on too much about dresses fitting properly on the shoulders, or had fits about zips getting stuck, like they'd started to do now.

But he was glad they were all fussing about that

at the moment because it meant he could do his wedding picture for school without getting nagged.

As soon as tea was over he settled himself peacefully at the smooth wooden table with his piece of paper and Pam's felt-tipped pens. He prayed that no one would interfere. He didn't dare look anywhere but at that paper in case something awful happened – like Rita bending over him with a dripping butter knife, or mam trailing coffee drips, or Albert coughing up a load of jam sandwich which had gone down the wrong way.

Then, like a miracle, Jonny seemed to have the whole room to himself with Razzle sitting quietly under his chair and the kitchen clock lying on its side on the mantelpiece ticking away – because it ticked best lying on its side.

He was half-way through his picture now. Humph had shown him how to draw a horse a little bit at a time. He made it brown, with a black flowing tail and a white bit like a little star on its forehead. "It even looks *slightly* like that one at our door . . ." he thought, proudly, as he added thick green lines of fresh green grass for it to munch. Nearly finished . . .

The room began to fill up again as Rita came in with a whole load of school books which she thumped on the table with the force of a meteor landing from outer space. He sighed as his paper was swept away on the breeze and pens rolled in all directions. Then he heard her say to the rest of them: "He hasn't finished that thing yet! What's it for anyway?"

"I think he's got to do it for school, love," said mam consolingly. "There's no need to be quite so impatient, Rita – he's done a very good brown and white teddy-bear on it. He seems to be better at drawing teddy-bears than any of you girls ever were. Perhaps his teacher'll put it on the wall." Mam beamed at everyone. She was beginning to feel proud, and peaceful. All the plans for Pat's wedding at St Anne's Church on Saturday were going like clockwork. The wedding cake was ready. It was three layers high with silver bells on it. The dresses were finished.

The wedding reception was going to be upstairs in the Arizona Street Church Assembly Rooms. Dale's mother Mrs Watkins was a very nice person and they got on well. Mrs Watkins said Dale couldn't have chosen a better girl than Pat! And Mrs Briggs said that Pat couldn't have chosen a better boy than Dale – even if they were too young and too mad on ice-skating. She and Mrs Watkins were sharing the reception costs. Sandra and Marilyn were making hundreds of salmon sandwiches and trifles, and Mrs Watkins was keeping them in the large freezer in her garage.

Suddenly, Jonny felt someone breathing heavily into his left ear. He put up his hand to try and blot them out. There was nothing worse than having someone leaning almost on top of you – snorting down your ear. His hand caught the tip of Rita's nose as she edged away quickly.

"It's not a teddy-bear, our mam, it's a brown and white billy-goat. Fancy him being able to copy a billy-goat at his age! Even I can't draw billy-goats." Like lightning a strong fist of fingers and a pincer-like thumb whipped the picture away to be displayed to all with cries of: "That's no more a billy-goat than a tortoise!" "Mam wants her eyes testing. It's certainly not a teddy-bear!" "Why would our Jonny want to draw a teddy-bear?"

Then, as Jonny sat there shrinking in his chair,

Albert said: "It's a monster with outer-space measles. The dreaded lurgi strikes again. It looks like a four-legged chair with stuffing falling out at one end."

"You just talk for the sake of talking, Albert," said mam.

"Albert's right in one way . . ." said Rita, beginning to enjoy herself, "they do make very funny chairs, these days. Chairs can look like horses or *anything*. But he should have given it fatter legs for a chair."

It was too much. Like a tornado, Jonny leapt towards Rita, and amid clattering chairs and crashing tables flung himself towards the back of her shoulders. She wasn't going to get away with *that*. He'd tried and tried to take no notice. But how could he, after all that? That picture was important. His own *horse*. And it looked like a horse, too. It was different when *mam* made mistakes because she wasn't wearing her glasses and she often made mistakes. But chairs, tortoises . . . BILLY-GOATS . . .?

"Ow . . . Gerroff . . ." bawled Rita in her loudest and most threatening tone. "He's nothing but a little vulture! Get him off me someone! He'll ruin my lace collar." Suddenly she fell backwards on top of Jonny and they both collapsed to the floor taking a chair and a bowl of fruit with them.

Shrieks and struggles, grunts, groans and sweating red-faced rage exploded as, sinkingly, he felt the full force of Rita's back-side on his head. Then he heard dad's voice say: "What the hell's going on? Those bananas'll be bruised to blazes!. They'll be no good for my bait box now. And just look at all those apples! And as for you miss –" glowering at Rita – "It's an all-in wrestler you'll need to be looking for when it comes to marriage."

Slowly Jonny clambered from underneath Rita. His nose was throbbing and there was a trace of blood on his lower lip where his tooth had jabbed it. But all the time his mind was on that precious piece of paper – his picture. Where was it now? He saw Rita standing there brushing her skirt and blouse indignantly as she stuck back a false eyelash. She was trying to ignore him completely.

But mam wasn't. "You naughty, naughty boy," she shouted. "Never let me see you attack poor Rita like that again! It's time that you learnt that girls don't expect behaviour like that. I've a good mind to give you a jolly good walloping . . ."

"But mam . . . she started it! She grabbed my drawing."

"I don't care who started it. It's up to you to behave properly. All you needed to do was to ask Rita politely to give it you back. Rita's beginning to grow into a young lady, now. And you don't have fights with young ladies. Not in *this* house."

So that was what Rita was, was it . . .? A young lady.

Jonny began to look angrily round for his drawing but there wasn't a sign of it. Supposing it had gone for good? What would he tell Miss Broom in the morning? It was no good him trying to do another one. He felt as if all the energy required for drawing pictures had suddenly vanished. He felt almost like a wet lettuce now, he was so shocked and disappointed and upset. He could feel tears starting to spurt into his eyes.

"Rita's not a lady, she's a spoilt, grabbing, mean, big-mouthed bum-face," he shouted as he rushed upstairs to his bunk.

Humph was there, reading a book. "Not another one crying," he said in amazement. "And what was all that thumping going on downstairs?"

With a half-smothered sob, Jonny told him about the drawing.

"It must be *somewhere*," said Humph, wrinkling his monkey brow. "It can't have vanished into thin air. The main thing is for it not to have slipped into some black and murky place like the back of the cooker, or into one of our Albert's shoes. Anyway, cheer up. If it's really disappeared I'll draw you another one."

Jonny shook his head. "They'd know I hadn't done it. It wouldn't be the same. And anyway, it wouldn't be on the right paper."

"Have a rest for a bit then. Wait till our Rita's got herself out to meet Mavis. Then, when it's all quietened down, I'll help you to look for it."

Jonny began to cheer up. He lay down on his bunk and began to read a comic. Perhaps things weren't as bad as he'd imagined.

As he lay there he heard Rita rushing upstairs to get ready to go out.

"And don't think I've forgotten being attacked, our Jonny!" she called, as a strong whiff of Midnight Sin scent almost choked him to death. "Don't imagine for one moment that you'll get away with an attack like that. It so happens that Mavis and I have got an urgent appointment with two supporters of World Peace tonight otherwise I'd have let you have it good and proper, on the spot." And with that she galloped down the stairs like a baby elephant and was off out.

Jonny sighed with a cold tremor of relief, and Humph muttered something about Rita changing her name to Deadly Nightshade. Then they both went downstairs.

The living-room was completely empty. Mam and Sandra were in the front-room talking about gold and silver paper doilies. They were making all the arrangements for the bouquets and buttonholes for the wedding, and gold and silver paper doilies were what they were going to arrange the pink carnations on, to make them look extra special.

Dad had escaped to Billingham to borrow his brother Jeff's Wedding Suit. He and Jeff were almost the same size so they shared the navy-blue chalk stripe suit for all special occasions. It had very wide trouser legs and dad called it a "Fifty-pence Tailor's Dream" because he once found fifty pence stuck in the turned up bits at the bottom of the trouser legs.

Quickly, Humph and Jonny began to search the room, looking in corners, under cupboards and behind chairs for the missing drawing. They even looked in the kitchen waste bin and under the vegetable rack.

"Not a sign of it," said Humph at last. "All I can think is that someone has deliberately chucked it out, or hidden it. And the two people guilty of those crimes are mam – for chucking things out – and Albert – for hiding things. P'raps we'd better go and look in the dustbin."

They went into the backyard to where the bin was standing next to a clump of dandelions. Gingerly, Jonny lifted the heavy black plastic lid. He hated dustbins. There was always a rotting cabbagy smell about theirs. It was full of ashes and old newspapers and laddered nylon tights and baked bean tins and dust from the vacuum cleaner.

He smiled slightly with relief. No. No sign of his drawing . . .

Then Humph said suddenly, "Where exactly was Rita standing when she grabbed it off you?"

"Next to the sideboard near the fruit bowl."

"Right. Then there's one place we didn't look, and it was right near to Rita."

They both went back to the sideboard. Humph pointed to something on the wall above it. It was a large, framed photo of dad holding the darts league cup. And behind that photo was a small tip of white paper sticking out . . .

"Don't bank on it," said Humph as he reached up to move the photograph, "it's only a chance . . ."

"It is!" said Jonny excitedly as his drawing floated to the floor. Then his heart fell, for it had some huge creases down the middle. Miss Broom would go mad! No one could possibly take a *creased* drawing to school.

"Don't worry about that," said Humph cheerfully. "Just leave it with me and I guarantee it'll be good as new in the morning . . . if not better." And he grinned a big, white, clear, toothy smile.

When Jonny went to bed that night, he lay there for a while wondering how Humph would get those awful creases out of his drawing. But he knew that if Humph said they would be gone in the morning, well – they would be.

And sure enough, as he got ready for school the next day, there was his drawing, lying on the sideboard waiting for him. All smooth and complete.

"It looks lovely doesn't it love?" said mam, as she gave his hair a quick comb – because she was having the week off work and hadn't to rush out. Then, putting on her proper glasses, she said: "I can see now that it's a beautiful horse you've done! It even looks a bit like our Pat's wedding horse, come to think of it. Shall I write the name Hurricane on the back of the picture – so you can tell Miss Broom?"

Jonny nodded in a daze of happiness as mam wrote the name in neat block letters on the back of his paper.

"I expect it was a bit of a shock when our Rita grabbed it," she said thoughtfully. "Our Rita can be very grabby indeed, at times." Then she frowned slightly: "But that doesn't mean you should have –"

"It was all creased, mam," said Jonny in a quick, urgent voice – to stop her saying any more. "It was behind that picture of the darts cup. Humph smoothed it out for me –"

"*He* smoothed it?" said mam, beginning to smile. "It was *me* that smoothed it, lovey. I was asked to iron it for you. So I ironed it when I was doing the

38

hankies and it came up like new. Off you go then."
She gave him an affectionate peck on the cheek and
gave his T-shirt a sharp tug as she tried to tuck it in
at the back.

As Jonny shot along Port Street to school, he felt
really happy. Mam was actually standing there,
smiling and waving to him as he turned the corner.
And she *knew* it was a horse, and had even *ironed* it

for him.

It was a sunny day. He hoped it would be sunny for their Pat's wedding as well.

"Has something nice happened?" said Pam as they hurried into school.

He began to tell Pam about the ironed picture. "Talk about *disappearing acts,*" he said.

But as they sat on the floor in the hall after the morning hymns, listening to Mr Badger making announcements – there was another disappearing act too. For the horseshoe on top of the cupboard had also vanished. And people were whispering and looking for Jonny Briggs . . .

3
Rita's Revenge

Miss Broom was holding up Jonny Briggs's drawing so that everyone in the class could see it. "This is a very good piece of work, it just shows what some people can do when they really try. It's a pity it couldn't have been done at the same time as everybody else's."

"It won't be fair if you put his on the wall, miss," called Josie as she accidentally-on-purpose gave her own desk a big shove so that the tremor reached Jonny's. "He's copied that horse, and he had more time than us. And he did it on different paper an' all. You can tell! It's smoother."

"It wasn't different paper," shouted Pam loyally, "it's been *ironed*." There was blank silence. Ironed

paper stopped even the twins in their tracks. But not
for long as Jinny piped up: "He's got that horseshoe
off Mr Badger's cupboard, Miss Broom." Then she
bit her lip as if she was sorry to have said it –
because she wasn't really sure.

Miss Broom frowned. "Is this true?" Before
Jonny could answer she walked to his desk: "Open
your desk."

"It's not true, miss. I've never even touched it!"

"It was him talking about it that started all the row yesterday, miss . . ." said Josie, her rosy cheeks puffed up with excitement and her eyes sparkling. "And we all know it was a special present to Mr Badger from Martin Canebender."

Miss Broom stood there staring into Jonny's desk and Jonny saw her face soften. The inside of his desk was bleak and bare with the wear and tear of countless years of ink, wax crayon, scratched words, chipped initials, faded toffee papers and a few dog-eared school books and scraps of loose paper with lots of crosses on and "See Me" written at the bottom in red. She closed the desk lid and went back to her table.

Jonny felt awful. He felt like a criminal. He felt as if no one really believed that he knew nothing about the horseshoe. He didn't know how he was going to face play-time, because he knew the twins would torment him about it the whole time. Then, to cap all his misery, Miss Broom didn't say any more about the horseshoe but instead of putting his drawing on the wall with all the rest of them, she gave it him back without another word and told him to put it away.

"I think we've just about had enough of weddings and horseshoes, now," she said. "So you can all turn to page twenty-seven in your Mathematical Problems books. We are all going to do the problem about measuring our school yard. We shall spend half an hour with our metre rulers measuring bits of the yard before play-time. Then, after play-time we shall work out our Mathematical Problem.''

Jonny cheered up a bit. He liked measuring the school yard. It was better than sitting there being got at, and you could talk while you worked. He usually worked with Pam because she was good at writing down the measurements.

When they were outside he said: "Do you think that horseshoe could have slipped down the back of Mr Badger's cupboard and got stuck? The way my picture got stuck at home?''

Pam looked up from her measuring. They were both measuring a little corner, well away from all the rest of the class. It was the spot closest to an old green door which Mr Box the caretaker kept shut when he drank his morning mug of tea and read the paper. But now the door was open because Mr Box was somewhere else. And through the open door there were lots and lots of silvery grey pipes showing.

"I don't think it slipped down the back of the cupboard," said Pam. "There's no space. Somebody must have taken it. But who . . .?''

They both stood up and stretched their legs as they tried to puzzle it out. The mild, hazy morning air was laced with home baking from the local apple-pie shop, along with traces of exhaust fumes from cars and buses. Birds twittered in the town dust and dogs scampered and played in the back streets. It was a quiet, happy morning.

Then, to their amazement and at exactly the same moment, they both saw something. It was just as if some fairy had waved a magic wand and stuck treasure in front of their very noses, there, on the floor, all on its rusting own, beneath a small bent coppery looking pipe . . .

"The HORSESHOE!" gasped Jonny. He let the metre ruler fall to the ground and hurried after Pam who was already inspecting their discovery.

"It's definitely the same one," she said – touching it gingerly with her little finger. "I can tell by its rusty colour and those three nobbly nail marks and that sharp bit of metal at the top."

Jonny screwed up his nose a bit. "What a funny place to put it," he said. "P'raps they pinched it and then flung it in here when they were escaping from Mr Badger. P'raps we'd better go straight away and tell him we've found it."

"P'raps we should take it with us," said Pam. "Because if *someone* has just dumped it while they were escaping from Mr Badger, *someone* might come back for it. And they might come back at play-time and take it away again. Then people would never believe us if we said it was here – lying on this floor."

Jonny hesitated. He was very glad they'd found the horseshoe, but quite frankly the less he had to do with it the better. As far as he was concerned it was the most unlucky horseshoe in the world. But Pam was already lifting it off the grey concrete floor and dusting it over with a paper tissue. "Do you want to carry it? Or shall I?"

"I'll carry it," said Jonny. "Seeing as how everyone was saying it was me . . . I hope no one spots us with it, though."

The bell for play-time was starting to ring as they gathered up their note-books, pencils and metre rulers from the yard and went towards the school entrance.

The effect was instantaneous. Every eye became magnetised by that lump of old iron that now lay clutched between Jonny's unwilling fingers.

"He's even been kicking it round the school yard with Pamela Dean instead of doing measuring," gabbled the twins to the Brown brothers, and about fifty others.

"I never saw them kicking it around," said Peter, cautiously.

"Because you're always so busy *working* you never see anything, dozy-face!" snapped Jinny scornfully. "It's pathetic the way you always try to stick up for those two. I'm going straight to Miss Broom to tell her."

But unfortunately Miss Broom had done a very quick dash to the corner shop – because the teachers' staff room had run out of coffee – and she was nowhere to be found.

Jonny and Pam stood timidly outside Mr Badger's door. Jonny gave a tiny knock, half hoping Mr Badger wouldn't be in.

"Come in!" bellowed a voice.

They both stood there transfixed. Mr Badger's voice sounded very bad-tempered indeed.

"Come *in*." The door swung open and Mr Badger himself stood there looking down at them with a slightly puzzled expression on his face.

"Have you come to see me about the school nurse

48

inspecting your ears?" he said. "What is it?"

"Please sir," said Jonny breathlessly, "we've found the horseshoe. It wasn't me who stole it, sir."

Mr Badger looked more puzzled than ever. "Come in for a minute," he said, sighing. "Now, what's all this about you stealing something?"

Jonny held up the horseshoe with quavery hands. "We found it, sir."

"Very good, very good," said Mr Badger, vaguely, as if he hadn't the slightest idea what it was all about.

"I didn't take the horseshoe away, sir. But Pam and me just found it."

"Took it away? Away from where?"

"From your cupboard outside, sir . . ." Jonny's voice was going dry and crackly.

"Please Mr Badger," said Pam, "you said it had gone off your cupboard in the corridor. You told us when we were in the hall this morning."

"So I did, so I did," said Mr Badger smiling the smallest flicker of a smile. "But one of the things you children must learn to do is to listen properly to what I have to say. I didn't say it had been stolen. I said it was *missing*. There is a great deal of difference between those two words."

Then, without another word, Mr Badger took the horseshoe from Jonny and offered each of them a digestive biscuit out of his special biscuit tin! Then he told them to "run along" before they missed the rest of their play-time.

"Fancy Mr Badger giving us a biscuit each!" said Pam, wiping the last bit of crumb from her mouth in astonishment. And then, as they walked into the yard, something even more astonishing happened. Mr Box appeared and he was frowning and wagging his finger at some of the boys in the top class. Then he started walking all round the school yard like a great big giant in his old black tank beret rubbing his hands together as if he was getting ready to have a fight with someone.

But he smiled a bit when he got near Pam and Jonny. "How's the gold belt going on?" he asked. "I could do with that gold belt myself this morning to bring me a bit of luck. Some little perisher's been and grabbed a very important piece of school equipment off the floor in the boiler room."

"Was it the shape of a sort of . . . a sort of horseshoe, Mr Box?" whispered Pam, looking up at him with big round eyes.

"Glory alleluia! You must be a little mind reader," he said, a smile appearing on his face. "Have you seen it somewhere?"

"Mr Badger told us a horseshoe was missing . . ." she didn't know what to say next . . . "Mr Badger said it was missing – off his cupboard . . ."

"Aye, that's right," said Mr Box, cheerfully. "I took it. I took it to use for propping up a real devil of a piece of copper piping. It's the bit linked to that rumbling clanking sound in the Headmaster's room. That horseshoe is going to be ideal for a great, hitching up, wedging, and bending of pipes process . . . accompanied by a few gentle taps with a large hammer. It's going to do the whole school a favour is that old horseshoe." Then he stopped suddenly and fixed them both with a sharp stern look: "So where is it now then? The quicker it's found – the more peace and light there'll be for all of us in the corridors of power . . ."

Jonny looked down at the ground helplessly: "We thought . . . well we saw it and took it to Mr Badger

". . . You see . . . we . . ." his voice faded.

Mr Box raised his big bushy eyebrows: "You *see*, says you. But you doesn't see at all . . ."

"We *thought* . . ." said Pam.

"You *thought*, did you?" said Mr Box dryly. "Whatever did I do to be saddled with such a load of Meddlesome Matties?" And he hurried off to see Mr Badger again.

"Thank goodness it wasn't really missing, and that you didn't get the blame, Jonny," said Pam when they were back in the classroom. "I'm glad Martin's horseshoe is helping the whole school like Mr Box said. It isn't often that Martin Canebender has a chance to help anyone."

Jonny nodded. He never wanted to see or hear of that lump of rusty old iron again, and he felt that if their Pat had any of those unmentionable monstrosities at her wedding he would get Razzle to run off with every one and dump them in the park pond.

"I wish I could be in a wedding with a horse and carriage," said Pam as they walked home from school that day. "You're ever so lucky, Jonny. I'll come and watch it all on Saturday, if you like."

"*You* can come and watch if you want," he said slowly, "but not all the rest. Peter could come as well if he wanted but he doesn't like weddings. If it rains it'll be best, then no one will watch. It'll be like being a monkey in the zoo if *some* people watch us."

Pam nodded sadly. Then she brightened up and said: "Will you be wearing your gold belt?"

He shook his head gloomily: "Pat doesn't like home-made gold belts unless they've been done on the sewing machine." Then, going pink all over with his final guilty secret, he said shame-facedly: "I'll be wearing long white velvet trousers with blue satin stripes up the sides, and a frilly shirt."

Pam's eyes shone with delight: "You lucky duck! You'll look as good as a pop singer!"

He began to feel better. "I never thought of that," he said.

There was a blanket of quietness over the house when he reached home. No voice yelling from inside. No backyard doors slamming. Not even the occasional excited yelp from Razzle. Yet, there was one very slight noise . . . at least he thought there was . . . Or was he just imagining it? Was it just because this special noise had been in their house for so long . . .?

It was the sound of the sewing machine. But the sound vanished almost before it started.

He ran in through the back door.

"Mam . . .?"

There was no reply. He didn't really expect one, because mam said she'd be out making last-minute arrangements.

He patted Razzle, then walked into the living-room.

Dead silence.

He went into the front-room where the sewing machine was. The lid was on it. All traces of wedding fever and marathon sewing sessions were gone. The sun shone silently against the curtains.

He ran upstairs to his bedroom. Was he imagining things?

He was just going to take his football out to play, when he heard a rustling noise. One small quiet rustle of paper from the girls' bedroom. Was it a mouse? Or had a bird flown in through an open window by mistake?

He crept from his own room and, very slowly and carefully, began to open the other bedroom door. It

took only the slightest fraction of an opening to tell him that someone was in there, as he caught sight of a purple painted toe-nail . . .

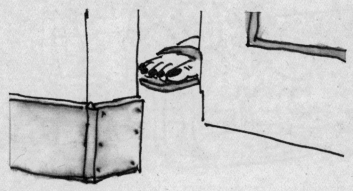

Rita! He closed the door quickly – expecting a shoe to land on him any minute, but nothing happened. What on earth was she up to? Why was she home from college so early?

Hastily he took his football and, with Razzle jumping about excitedly by his side, he went to the park to play.

That evening, after tea, mam said: "I want you all to do a dress rehearsal for the wedding. I want everyone – dad and all – to put on their wedding things just for a final check-up to make sure we don't all turn out looking like a rag-bag on Saturday."

"You can count me out for a start, our mam," said Rita with amazing haste. "Mavis and I have got better things to do than that. Mavis and I are organising a clog-kicking contest in aid of World Peace with these two students who are studying the history of clogs and clog-dancing. Mine is very tall with piercing brown eyes and he can't stand people who are late for appointments." In a flash Rita had vanished down the street wearing a bright red skirt covered in massive embroidery stitches done very quickly with a darning needle and some thick knitting wool.

Mam sighed resignedly. "Trust her not to be helpful," she said. "All I hope is that when Saturday arrives she doesn't wear a pair of clogs with her blue silk bridesmaid's dress." Then she said, "Where's Albert? He was here a second ago."

But Albert had gone too, and even Humph discovered he had to dash off to the library.

"I'll join you, too, lad," said dad with a panic-stricken look on his face. "There's a book on cabinet making I wanted to look up."

Until in the end there were only two people left – Jonny and his mother.

"Better than nothing, I expect," said mam. "I must be thankful for small mercies. I'll get your outfit. P'raps it's as well there's no one else here to torment us. It's always best to have a dress rehearsal rather than waiting till the actual day."

She went in the front-room and brought out a large loosely wrapped package stuffed with tissue paper. Carefully she unwrapped the white velvet suit and waited whilst Jonny got ready to slip into the trousers.

"I'll hold them for you love, so as they won't fall on the floor or get creased," said mam in her kindest voice. Jonny balanced against her and put a small bare foot into the long, tubular, velvet trousers and hopped about slightly on his other leg.

Then, he suddenly stopped hopping about and balancing, and almost fell over in frustration, as mam began to stare at him irritably.

"There's no need to make such a *meal* of it, son," she said sharply. "No one can say that they aren't wide enough to get into! I was most careful to make sure that –"

"It's the bottoms, mam. The end bit . . ." Jonny took his foot out of one leg and tried the other one and again he came to a full stop. "It's just like putting your foot in a narrow paper bag, our mam." He began to look indignant. Weddings were a load of rubbish. All the others had managed to escape, and here he was, completely trapped, when he could have been out playing. Trapped, with his leg in a long white velvet funnel.

"Get out of them then, and let's have a look," said mam. She was beginning to get really tetchy, and deep lines appeared, between her eyebrows. Then, as Jonny stood there waiting, she put her own arm down one of the legs and came to a full stop: "*Someone . . . someone* has machined the bottoms so you can't get your feet through!" she exclaimed. She flopped down in a chair in exhausted disbelief, all the joy and peace of plans working like clockwork vanishing into thin air. "Put the kettle on, our Jonny, and make me a cup of tea before I collapse."

Quickly, Jonny put some water in the kettle. This was the first time he had ever been allowed to make a cup of tea in the whole of his life (usually mam said it was too dangerous and she didn't want any accidents). But he knew how to do it off by heart. With great care he put the kettle on the gas stove and two tea bags in mam's smallest tea-pot. Then he put some milk in her cup with the bluebell border.

"I'll do the rest," said mam, suddenly reviving as she poured the boiling water into the pot. "You need to be a bit taller yet – before you do that part."

"Who ever could have done such an unkind trick as that?" said mam. As she sipped her tea she looked at the small rows of machine stitches. Those stitches will take hours to undo! I shall have to unpick each one separately. What a cruel joke . . . I wonder if it was one of our Albert's ridiculous ideas?" Then she shook her head: "No . . . I can't see Albert being able to machine a straight line on anything. And Humph would never *dream* . . . or the girls . . ." Suddenly she took a huge gulp of tea. Jonny's eyes met hers and quickly he said: "Give us your tea-cup mam and I'll go and wash it up for you!"

"Stay right where you are," said mam briskly as the whole plot began to dawn. "It's obvious now, who did this. It was our Rita taking revenge on you for attacking her when she had your picture. I told you you were a naughty boy at the time – and now

look what's happened! As usual it's me that has to suffer in the end. Just wait till that young madam gets back . . . just *wait!*"

Furiously, mam began to unpick all the machine stitching Rita had so busily provided, and as she did so, her cheeks got redder and redder and her temper grew and grew as she went on and on about all the hard work of preparing for a wedding. Jonny would have liked to have slipped out of the back door – but he just didn't dare. Instead he just stood next to her and kept saying "yes mam" and "no mam" and "thank you, mam", until the stitching was all out while he dreamed, secretly, of a desert island, away from it all . . .

Finally mam said: "Now try them on . . ." This time everything went like clockwork, and he looked such a little angel – all glowing and anxious to please – that her heart melted completely.

But when she had packed the outfit away again in the front-room she said: "I can't allow our Rita to get away with this, Jonny. I know you were partly to blame but what she did was beyond a joke. Just imagine if we had only found out when we were setting off on Saturday – it could have ruined the whole wedding and caused a fiasco we'd have remembered to the end of our lives!" Then she said: "Anyway, you'd better get out to play for a bit. This is a matter for me and Rita to settle."

What a relief! Jonny shot out of the house like a bird from a cage. Freedom at last! Perhaps it would

all blow over after all. P'raps mam and Rita would
get it sorted out when nobody else was there.

But when he was getting ready for bed that night
he heard Rita coming in with her friend Mavis. At
first he tried to blot out the noise by hiding under
the covers but it was impossible. So he crept out of
bed and sat on the stairs to listen instead.

4
The Awful Row . . .

The noise of the row was awful. Jonny could hear every word of it. And even before that, when he was in mam and dad's room looking through their bedroom window to see if there was any sign of Rita getting back, he'd heard her as well as seen her.

Rita had said: "Don't go off and leave me *now*, Mavis. You may as well come in, so as mam and dad'll know I'm speaking the truth about the clog-kicking contest lasting longer than we thought."

Then Jonny had heard Mavis saying nervously: "I always get the feeling your dad doesn't like the sound of our bracelets rattling, Rita. Anyway, I'm supposed to take this load of fish and chips back piping hot for Granny and Grandad."

"It'll only be for a *second*, Mavis. The chips'll soon warm up again in the oven. Tell them to use *oven* chips in future."

"But they don't like them! They like proper ones. They've always been very kind to me, Rita. It was Grandad who first gave me the pliers and wire cutters for making wire jewellery."

Jonny had heard the door open as they went inside. It was quiet for a few minutes but now trouble was really on the boil, and Rita's voice rang out: "If you all expected me to let that little wrecker attack me and not do a thing about it you had another think coming! Mavis and I are sick to death of him! The number of friends we've lost through them knowing he's my brother is enormous. Those two Bingo checkers on holiday from Nottingham last week fled when our Jonny came up to us in broad daylight and told me mam wanted me to get her an extra pound of sausage from Tesco's. Mine

said his train was due any minute and Mavis's said he had to get his shoes from the repairer's.''

"I am not interested in Bingo callers from Nottingham, Rita!" shouted mam excitedly. "What I'm interested in is the cruel and thoughtless way you machined up the bottoms of those wedding pants of our Jonny's and left *me* to undo them all.''

"Well, you shouldn't have undone them should you, mam? You should have left them for *him* to undo and it would have taught him a lesson.''

"Talk sense, Rita! How could anyone else have unpicked those tiny stitches without making everything look a complete mess?''

"You should have just cut the bottoms off with a pair of scissors, mam,'' shouted Albert, "and let him go as Robinson Crusoe.''

"With *me* made the laughing stock of the whole of Middlesbrough!" shrieked Pat. "It's going to be bad enough as it is, having Dale's stuck-up little cousin there dressed the same as our Jonny. It'll show us up even more, if anything goes wrong.''

Jonny blinked in the moonlit darkness. Dale's cousin? Dressed the same as him? It was the first time he'd heard that mentioned. In a way he felt pleased. It was better having two people looking a bit daft than one. Then Jonny heard dad thunder: "Look everyone, I'm damned well pig sick of this wedding! The sooner Saturday's over the better. I don't want to hear another word from anyone – is that understood?''

"You'll never hear *me* mention it again," screamed Pat, "because I'm off this minute to stay with our Marilyn, and I never, never, want to come in this house again! Mam can bring my dress round there and I'll get the horse and carriage sent there instead. Dad needn't try and give *me* away at the wedding either. I'd sooner ask the milkman."

"If you're going, I'd better come with you, to look after you," said Sandra. "I'm not having all my cooking arrangements mucked up by everyone going off their nut. P'raps by tomorrow there'll be a bit more sense around."

Then there was a great slamming of doors and rushing off into the night air, and Jonny heard Rita shout dramatically: "And *I* am going right now to live with Mavis at her house for ever, so there! Come on Mavis . . ."

"It can only be for tonight, Rita, because of Aunty Molly coming to stay," said Mavis quickly.

Jonny went back to his bedroom. At least it would make a change having none of the girls at home. Just dad and the boys, and mam to look after them, what bliss! Then he heard mam's voice bellow: "That's it! If I don't get away for one night – I'll go off my beam-end."

"You go, love," said dad. "You've had a raw deal from that gang. It's amazing what we've managed to bring into this world between us. Go to your mother's for a . . ."

"Don't you tell *me* what to do," said mam. "Mrs Watkins said if things got too much for me she would gladly accompany me on a night out to a hotel of our choice. Dale's mother is a woman after my own heart." And with that, mam too departed, with a loud slam of the door.

A minute or two later, Jonny heard dad going slowly to bed, all on his own. Then Humph and Albert came upstairs, all quiet and subdued.

Jonny shut his eyes and pretended to be asleep. He was praying and praying for the wedding to be over. Then he heard Humph say: "They'll all be back tomorrow, you mark my words, Albert."

And Albert said: "I flippin' well hope so. They can't expect *us* to do cleaning and cooking and all that boring stuff."

Then the whole house lapsed into complete and utter sleepy silence, as if waiting to see what would

really happen in the morning.

The next morning when Jonny woke up he was absolutely amazed to hear his mother's voice talking away to dad as she cooked the breakfast.

"P'raps it was as well it was too late to go with Mrs Watkins to a hotel of my choice," she was saying. "Anyway, I had a very nice couple of hours at the Smilers Club. You should have been there, love. There was this enormous man who could rip

69

up telephone directories, and the midnight pie and peas was delicious."

Then dad said: "It's a good job I took these few days off, before this dreaded wedding. What shall we do about them all? Shall I go and round them up? Personally, I think it's easier without them."

"They'll come round without water," said mam. "Our Marilyn'll see to that. And as for Rita . . ."

Her voice was lost as violent hammering noises at the back door were followed by Rita rushing in to collect her school books and eye make-up. "I've decided to come back again for the time being, you'll be glad to know," said Rita. "But let this be a warning to you both. The next time I might go for good."

"Next time – make it Timbuctoo, our Rita," Jonny heard Albert say.

And he stayed safely upstairs until the door slammed behind Rita and he heard her high heels tottering down the street.

When Jonny set off for school he felt as if he could hardly wait to get Friday over and done with – so that Saturday could be over and done with as well. And when he got home again, the whole house was awash with wedding preparations.

Pat and Sandra were chattering away about how wedding veils should be worn, as if they'd never been out of the place. Then Sandra began to go over all the feeding arrangements at the Arizona Street Church Assembly Rooms whilst Albert kept butting in. Until finally he said: "And watch out no one gets salmonella food poisoning! You've got to be very careful with chicken. I once read about a wedding where fifty people spewed up."

And mam roared at him: "Get out this minute, Albert! I just can't stand it!"

"What's all this about Dale's cousin, our mam?" said Jonny as he slipped once again into his white velvet wedding suit and found it fitted perfectly.

"You and him have to walk together down the aisle behind Dale and me," said Pat glaring at him. "And mind there's no monkey tricks. He's been very well brought up. He's coming from fifty miles away specially for Dale's wedding, and they're so rich that they travel abroad to watch the World Cup. Anyway . . . he's a bit older than you, our Jonny, so he'll be able to keep you right."

Jonny felt his heart sink: "What's his name?"

"Granby."

"Granby? Is that his *first* name?" Jonny's heart sank even lower. He would have felt much happier if he'd been called Craig, or Gareth, like people at school.

"You and him are supposed to keep my veil from blowing away," said Pat, positively scowling.

Jonny wondered how on earth Dale had ever wanted to marry Pat – she looked so bad-tempered with her hair in big blue rollers ready for tomorrow and white grease all over her face. When she and Dale had gone ice-skating she used to look pretty in

all those ice-skating skirts that mam made. She'd
had quite a kind expression – but now she only
needed next-door's tom cat and she'd be a regular
witch . . . Without thinking, and quite out of the
blue, some words fell from Jonny's lips: "Will you
take your broomstick tomorrow, our Pat?"

"Whatever is that supposed to mean, you . . .?"

"Sorry – I meant – you know – something *old*."

"I know what he means," said mam hastily as she
sensed another blow-up, "he means 'something old,
something new, something borrowed, something
blue', don't you, love?"

"Yes, mam," he smiled gratefully.

"Well, all that remains now," said mam, "is for
us all to keep calm till the great 'tomorrow' actually
arrives. Me, Humphrey and Albert will travel in Mr
Coxley's taxi, and we'll go first, so as Albert and
Humphrey can give out the hymn books and

arrange everyone. After that the horse and carriage will collect dad and Pat. And that will be followed by the wedding car with Rita and Sandra and our Jonny in it, and Aunty Iris who'll be here first thing in the morning. So there shouldn't be any trouble over that, should there? It's all quite straightforward."

Everyone nodded their heads. Mam was queen of all she surveyed.

"We'd better get an early night then," she said, as they all tottered nervously upstairs to bed. "We're all going to need every scrap of energy for tomorrow. The weather forecast on the television said it was going to be sunny and warm with occasional odd showers and breezy in places – so we'll all have to keep our fingers crossed. Goodnight, loves."

"It's quite an adventure really, having a wedding, isn't it Humph?" said Jonny as he climbed into his bunk.

"This one probably will be," said Humph. "So let's get off to sleep sharp. This one's been enough to last me a hundred years."

"A thousand years ..." said Albert sleepily. Then he suddenly sat up and said in a loud voice: "Are we taking the dog? He can sit next to me in the taxi." Then he flopped down again. And soon they were all fast asleep.

But as Jonny slept, a voice seemed to be saying: *Razzle. You must take Razzle! You can't leave him out ...*

5
The Wedding

The main thing Jonny heard when he woke the next morning was the sound of rain pattering heavily on the roof.

He was the very first to be up.

The words about taking Razzle to the wedding were still buzzing in his brain. If Razzle *was* allowed to come, he would have to be spick and span, and smell nice – just as if he was at the special pet show again.

Jonny slipped out of the back door to take stock of Razzle.

The rows and rows of dark-blue slate roofs shone with summer showers, and the air had a bouncing, refreshing mischief in it as watery drops plopped

steadily from gutters to puddles and from backyard walls to cabbages, around Razzle's kennel.

Jonny stared thoughtfully at him. Razzle's paws were all yellowy and his coat was rough and spiky looking from romping in some mud yesterday. He looked *dreadful!*

As quickly as he could, Jonny got an old plastic bucket, filled it with warm soapy water, and gave Razzle a real "going over". Then he brushed and combed him on the kitchen step and, grabbing him tightly, hauled him upstairs as quietly as possible to the bedroom so as he'd keep clean till it was time to go.

Razzle's tail was wagging like anything. And in a flash he was razzling about happily at the end of Jonny's bunk.

"*Now* what is it?" groaned Albert with his eyes still tightly shut. "Can't we ever get any proper peace in this house?"

"Albert . . ." whispered Jonny cautiously . . . "you know that Magpie's Rosette that Uncle Derek once gave us, from the old days? Where is it?" His voice was hoarse with urgency as he prayed that Albert would answer him reasonably and not suddenly shoot up like a rocket and start everyone off on the wrong foot, by arguing about football rosettes and the chances of Newcastle ever being top of the league again. And whether Boro was ten times better.

"Magpie's Rosette? How should I know? It was years ago! Shut up."

"But I know where it is, Albert. It's stuck between the covers of your *Big Book of Magic*. It'll be just right for Razzle to wear for the wedding – because it's black and white, like him."

Albert opened his eyes wide: "Don't say you've got *him* in here! I thought there was a strange pong."

"It's dad's new scenty foam shave –"

"Heck, our Jonny, surely you didn't use it on Razzle? Dad'll go wild!"

"Only a bit . . . can I, Albert?"

"Can you *what?*"

"Have that Magpie's Rosette?"

"Do what you like. Only leave me in peace, before all the suffering starts later on."

Delightedly, Jonny fastened the huge rose-like, black and white, frilly ribbon to Razzle's collar. Razzle accepted it placidly.

"He seems really proud of it, Albert . . ."

The concentrated din of three alarm clocks drowned any reply, and mam's voice began to fill the air as people flopped out of bed and plodded blearily to the bathroom.

Breakfast that morning was a skimpy affair. Even dad didn't eat much as he stared like a man struck dumb at the transformation of the Briggs family. One by one they changed from what seemed to be a set of sluggish, dull-coloured chrysalids, into shimmering butterflies – like Albert in his shining white shirt, spanking purple tie, and immaculate grey suit.

"Crikey," gasped Humph, as he put on a pair of new blue socks, "our dad looks like a lord in that suit of Uncle Jeff's. The waistcoat actually buttons up, an' all."

"And you look like a lord's son, Humphrey," said mam. "I've never seen you looking so neat in all my life. I like you much better with your hair a bit shorter and a proper parting in it." Then she said anxiously: "I hope that isn't a brick in your jacket pocket, love. We were only kidding when we said we'd have to wedge the church door open."

"It's a camera, mam. A flat, folding one. Forty years old. I got it at a jumble sale."

"Don't expect me to stand there while you try to get *that* to work," said Pat. "Dale and I will have a professional photographer."

Jonny blinked at her in a magical daze. She looked *beautiful*. Her hair shone in soft waves and her eyes were dark blue and glowing like the deep inside of velvety flowers. Her dress was a mass of flowing white lace that seemed to be full of creamy butterflies. And it was gathered up round the waist like layers and layers of soft white cloud in a clear blue sky.

"Stop gawping at me, our Jonny," said Pat, "and get into your velvet suit. The horse and carriage'll be here in a few minutes."

Silently he allowed mam to help him into his outfit, then stood completely still. Sandra and Rita were waiting stiffly by his side in their long blue silk bridesmaids' dresses, their gloved hands clutching nervously at the silver-wrapped stems of bouquets of scenty pink carnations.

Rita, miraculously pale and speechless, was wearing hardly any eye-liner because she didn't want to smear anything.

"You've got a family to be proud of," said Aunty Iris. Then she brushed the back of her hand across her eyes and said: "My eyes keep on watering something awful today. It's all the grit blown up by the wind," and she smiled at mam and dad.

Jonny could hardly wait for Hurricane and the black pram carriage to arrive. It was awful just

standing here all quiet and "done up" listening to
the clock ticking away . . . until . . . he remembered
Razzle . . .

He glanced at Albert, wondering whether to whis-
per anything, but Albert was in another world as he

stood there staring straight ahead like a soldier on sentry duty.

"It's not going to be a good thing to mention Razzle to *anyone*," thought Jonny.

"IT'S HERE!" shouted mam. "Come on you boys. I can hear Coxley's taxi . . ."

"It's that two-star petrol he uses," said dad glumly.

Hastily mam shepherded Albert and Humph to the front door and then Jonny was left with dad, Pat, Rita, Sandra and Aunty Iris.

The next thing was a knock at the door as the wedding car for Rita, Sandra, Jonny and Aunty Iris arrived, and Jack who was driving it came in and had a lump of home-made butterscotch whilst he reassured Pat that Hurricane would be arriving any second.

"We'll let you go first in the horse and carriage," he said to dad and Pat. "Then we can keep an eye on things from behind . . . for safety's sake and all that." Then, giving a big comfortable suck on the lump of butterscotch, he said to Pat: "Cheer up love, you look as if you're going to flake out."

"I have no intention of flaking out!" said Pat sparkily. "It was just you saying 'for safety's sake', as if there was going to be some sort of danger somewhere . . ."

Jonny ran to the front door and looked at the large dark-blue wedding car. Jack had thoughtfully opened the back door ready for them all to get in.

"Fancy him doing that in *our* street," thought Jonny staring. "Anything could happen! Someone might pinch all the plastic flowers. And what if next door's tom-cat hid under the seat . . .?" Then he hesitated as an idea suddenly struck him.

What if a small dog with a black and white rosette should hide under the seat? Trembling with excitement and even a trace of terror in case his plan didn't work and he was caught in the act, he trod quickly upstairs – missing all the squeaky bits – and with no more ado grabbed Razzle and put his hand warningly on top of Razzle's nose, which meant *silence*.

With a thumping heart he was downstairs again in seconds and out to the wedding car, and he tipped Razzle under the back seat. It was a big old-fashioned car and it wasn't boxed in at the bottom like modern ones. So there was quite a large gap where things could get lost under the big white wedding sheets which draped everything.

Razzle, like the good, well-trained, intelligent animal he was, lay there quiet as a happy log under the white sheets along the bottom of the back seat of the car.

"Where did you suddenly go off to?" said Rita when he returned to the room. "We don't want you mucking up everything by suddenly disappearing at the last minute."

"I only went upstairs," he said truthfully.

"Well, you can just go upstairs again then, and bring me my gold chain necklace out of the top

dressing-table drawer because I've decided to wear it. Seeing as how we're waiting so long."

Obediently Jonny ran upstairs again to get Rita's necklace. For once he was happy to help her. He liked her gold necklace. She looked good in it. It was almost as good as his gold belt. So if she had suddenly decided to wear her gold necklace, why shouldn't he wear his gold belt after all? White velvet was just right for gold belts.

Swiftly, he went back in his own bedroom and rooted out his gold belt from under the comics. It was slightly crumpled, but as he put it on, it straightened out and glowed and sparkled. And the minute he did it, he felt on top of the world. He felt all set for a proper occasion, for a world of celebration and magic and adventure.

He scampered downstairs again. And not a second too soon, because at last the sound of horse's hooves could be heard as Pat's carriage came to the front door followed by a general gathering of curious friends, neighbours and well-wishers, who stood round with stunned expressions.

With great solemnity, Pat and dad were ushered into the carriage by Jack's friend who was Hurricane's driver, and who wore a top hat for the occasion.

Then Jack ushered Rita, Sandra, Jonny and Aunty Iris into the big wedding car behind the carriage.

Luck was on Jonny's side. For a start no one even noticed his gold belt glowing round his waist. But

more important by far was the sound of Rita's voice asking Jack if she could sit next to him at the front.

"Wouldn't the little lad like to sit next to me?" said Jack, looking at Rita with a mixture of fear and doubt. "Bridesmaids usually sit in comfort at the back."

"Oh no, not all of them. I always like to sit next to the driver. I'd much sooner be next to you. It must be a terrible bore for you without someone on your own wavelength to talk to." Rita's smile was radiant and her eyelashes seemed to flutter like a line of black stockings caught in a gale.

"What do you think, sonny?" said the trapped Jack, praying that this sensible little lad in the white velvet uniform would protect him.

"Oh no, Jack. I'd *like* our Rita to sit at the front with you! She's good at telling people the right way to go."

Quickly he scrambled to the corner of the big, white back seat. He put his feet protectively over a large portion of Razzle; his Aunty Iris was next to him and Sandra in the other corner.

Jonny was right about Rita. No sooner had they set off than she was nagging on about short cuts along the back streets to Jack.

"We can't take short cuts, petal," said Jack good-humouredly. "We've got to follow closely behind my mate and that horse . . ."

Jonny bent forward and peered between Jack and Rita. He could see the small wedding carriage bobbing away among the Saturday morning traffic as they wove a mysterious route along the back of Woodlands Road.

"We seem to be going a very long way round, to St Anne's Church," said Aunty Iris. She had drunk a glass of sherry just before they came out and didn't really mind if they went via the North Pole.

But Rita wasn't quite so complacent. "It's turned

up Boro Road the wrong way!" she gasped. "It's trotting away from the town centre! It's *galloping* towards Marton Road, and if it gallops like that for long enough we'll all be on Roseberry Topping within an hour. Jack! You must overtake them and tell them to stop!"

"Chance is a fine thing," groaned Jack as they halted at the traffic lights and wound their way slowly round a diversion caused by road works.

Then Sandra said calmly: "The only sensible thing to do will be for us to go straight to the church from here. Then at least we'll be able to warn everyone that they're galloping off in the wrong direction. All I hope is that they haven't gone for ever. I don't fancy bunging all that food back in the freezer."

With great dignity, Jack gave in and drove towards the church. And as Jonny sat there he saw all the people standing at the church gates watching the wedding and waiting for the bride.

"The Brown brothers are there," he muttered angrily with a sinking heart. "And the twins . . ."

"How nice for you, dear," said Aunty Iris. "What loyal little school pals you've got!"

Then Jonny saw Pam and Peter, and he waved, and they waved back, and he felt better.

As they emerged from the car – with Jack standing there holding the door open – Jonny was careful to let Aunty and the girls get well clear before he even set foot on the worn slabs leading to the church steps.

"Come on, sonny," said Jack. "You can't sit on my taxi seat for ever. I know Coxley's are the height of luxury and comfort, but this is ridiculous . . ."

Luckily, just at that moment, Jack caught the eye of Billy Binns who took proper wedding photographs and strolled across to tell him the sad tale of the disappearing bride.

Like magic, Jonny was out of the car with Razzle close by his side. They almost flew up the church steps and vanished behind the wooden door with its great black iron hinges.

Inside the church the air was soft and soothing with a background of gently played organ music and there were flowers everywhere, and rows of people in their best clothes. Then Jonny saw the worried faces of mam, Mrs Watkins, two very tall bridesmaids in primrose yellow dresses, a boy dressed just like him – who was obviously Granby – and Albert and Humph. They were huddled in a dark little corner at the back of the church next to a pile of red hymn books and a wooden collection box.

And at that moment – for some unknown and inexplicable reason – there was a sudden loud blast from the organ and the organist charged into a brisk rendering of *Here Comes the Bride*.

The effect on Razzle was dynamic! It was as if the whole mystery of his past life was now revealed – for surely he *must* have been a circus dog at one time. Only a musically-minded and precision-trained creature could have captured the glory of this unique occasion as – with a dignity and power equal only to that of Nebuchadnezzar the ancient Babylonian king – he began to walk slowly down the aisle all on his own, while people cast nervous side glances to see what the blushing bride looked like.

Jonny was frozen with horror! Razzle was already half-way towards the altar and he could see Mr Fotheringay the vicar in his long white surplice pointing his finger back towards the door and telling Razzle to GO. Jonny waited no longer. In one last fit of terror he turned and fled from the church to the outside steps wondering whatever to do next.

No one would ever forgive him for this for the rest of their days. It might even be in the *Evening Gazette* – then the whole school would know as well!

Perhaps if he set off right now to run all the way to

Land's End in aid of a good cause – so that they advertised *that* instead . . . *Picture of brave Jonny Briggs and his blistered feet after his seven-hundred-mile run to Land's End in aid of the church Organ Fund.*

Yes, that truly, was his only escape.

He had just started to run to the church gate when he heard someone running after him and a voice called: "Ha . . . wayyy . . . slow down a bit." He turned anxiously and saw that it was the boy dressed like himself – except that Granby hadn't got a gold belt, and he was tall with curly hair.

"Where a' you off to then?" said Granby. "Was it your dog? Is he a Newcastle supporter? Away the lads . . ."

Jonny stared at Granby. He didn't look very posh. He looked quite normal.

"I've decided to do a charity run to Land's End. Our mam and dad'll kill me . . . and our Pat'll probably blame me for ever, for spoiling her wedding."

Granby grinned: "But they aren't here yet. They won't know! That horse they hired was running for home. They say inside they'll be here in another five minutes."

Then Granby said: "Isn't it awful at weddings? But I like your gold belt. I wish I'd got one. Our lot'd never let us wear something as unusual as that." They both smiled in silent sympathy. Then Granby went on: "When you'd gone, the vicar actually patted your dog. He's taken him into that place they call the vestry. He likes animals. The minute after he'd shouted 'go' at it, and it didn't work, he shouted 'stay' – and after that it did everything he wanted. Did you train it yourself?"

Jonny nodded: "Me and my friend Pam trained

him. He's very clever. I brought him 'cos I knew
he'd like coming to a wedding." Jonny felt happier
now. He knew that Granby was his friend and some-
how he began to think that running all the way to
Land's End just for the organ fund was a bit too
much to do.

As they stood there under the big trees by the
church gate Jonny suddenly heard the sound of
horse's hooves clloppeting away in the distance.
Then Hurricane and the carriage appeared in the
distance and an excited cheer went up from the
crowd. Jonny felt quite proud. They were actually
cheering his sister!

In minutes, Pat and dad were struggling eagerly
from their galloping prison with very blushing faces
indeed. With equal eagerness Jonny took his place

behind them both, close to Pat's veil, and with Granby at his side, slowly and majestically they walked back into the church.

And this time when the organ played *Here Comes the Bride* everything went like clockwork. All the mothers cried because the bride looked so beautiful. Dale couldn't find the ring and almost fainted with panic when the best man unhooked it from his key ring. Razzle watched the wedding certificate being signed and was allowed to come back down the aisle with Jonny. And mam and Mrs Watkins put on such a spread in the Arizona Street Church Assembly Rooms that it is still talked about to this day.

As for Pat and Dale, they went happily off on a mystery honeymoon to Iceland with about a hundred coke tins clattering on the back of the car. And Humph's pictures of the wedding with his forty-

year-old camera turned out better than the so-called "proper ones".

"Your wedding was great, Jonny," breathed Pam when they were in the school yard on Monday morning. "I wish we could have a wedding like that in our family."

Jonny looked round the school yard. The twins were skipping at the other end. The Brown brothers were racing about near the gate. No one had come to torment him – which showed there was nothing they could find to torment him about.

Suddenly his face flooded into a big, happy smile. "It was a bit of a galloping wedding – but it all turned out right in the end," he said slowly.

Then he said: "Race you" – and they both chased like the wind in a great gust of joy.

The British School of Osteopathy

* 2 6 6 3 *

**This book is to be returned on or before
the last date stamped below.**

24 MAR 1983   1 0 MAY 1988

20 APR 1983   2 / OCT 1988

16 MAY 1983

24 JAN 1984

18 NOV 1985

27 NOV 1985

16 MAY 86

16 JUN 1986

24 FEB 1987

28 SEP 1987

SCHIÖTZ & CYRIAX

MANIPULATION
PAST and PRESENT